WHITE OAKS - A TOWN WITH NO LAW

U.S. Marshal Shorty Thompson

Paul L. Thompson

Longhorn
Publishing

FOREWORD

White Oaks New Mexico Territory was in Lincoln County, where Pat Garrett was county sheriff. The only thing wrong with that, Pat's office was in Lincoln, some forty miles away. Though Billy the Kid and his gang were long gone, rustlers, robbers, and killers haunted this rich gold town every night of the week.

Belle La Mar's Little Casino Saloon is where dozens of them hung out. The No Scum Allowed Saloon just up the street was the safest saloon for locals that just wanted to have a drink and talk.

A gang of better than twenty cut-throat outlaws gave the only deputy one hour to get out of town, which he did, leaving the town with no law.

CHAPTER ONE

After gold was found in the Jicarilla Mountains of Central New Mexico Territory, a tent city quickly grew into the bustling town of White Oaks, a ruthless, gambling, money grubbing town. The more gold that was discovered the larger the town grew. Several saloons, two liveries, a saw mill, grocery stores, butcher shops and so on. A bustling town of hundreds of people where outlaws saw this as a place to rob miners, drink and raise hell.

When they came to town, they quickly found the saloon to go to was Belle La Mar's Little Casino. Even the one town deputy was never seen in that rough place. He was afraid of being shot.

The town merchants besieged the mayor to hire a full-time sheriff to keep the riff raff out of their town. The only law was young James Redman, appointed deputy sheriff by Pat Garrett. "Henry, all James is going to do is mess around and get himself killed. One man alone cannot stand up to all the outlaws that converge in our town every blasted night. It is un-safe for women, children and yes even business men to be out on the streets after dark. Something has to be done."

Another man said, "Just the other day in broad daylight, that little Wanda Jorden came into town for groceries and was accosted again as she loaded those groceries. Bless her heart, scared her most to death.

With torn dress she jumped in that buggy and rode off with those men laughing their heads off. Arnold came into town with his guns looking for those men. Thank God, he didn't find them or he would be dead."

"Gentlemen don't blame me I have run adds in every newspaper for a month trying to find someone stupid enough to take the job. Perhaps an armed committee of several men could do the job. They could walk the streets at night and check in saloons for…"

"What you're saying is you want us to get into a gun-fight with a bunch of outlaws and get ourselves killed. Henry we are businessmen, not gun hands. You send a letter to the governor letting him know our situation. If these robberies and murders are not brought under control, it will be the end of White Oaks. Our wives will make us all sell out and leave this lawless town. White Oaks will become known as the town with no law. Mark my words no one will come here, people will move out."

The mayor looked at them. "I'll send a rider over to Lincoln and ask Pat Garrett to come over so we can talk. If only we could get him to stay in town a week… Just one week might make the difference and show these outlaws what they are doing will not be tolerated."

"You know what I think Henry?"

"No, what?"

"I think you are full of crap! Pat Garrett don't give ah damn about White Oaks or this would have already been taken care of. James rides over and talks with him twice a month. Don't you think he has told Pat numerous times of what is going on around here and he can't handle it? You get in touch with the governor or by damn we will!"

Another man said, "I know! I have a friend that is now a U.S. Marshal out of Denver. I'll ride over to Socorro and send a wire to his boss Captain Long. I am sure he will give us a hand. Just one or two marshals is all we would need."

The mayor looked at him. "Good Heavens Delbert, you're too old to make such a trip unless you take the stage."

"I'm not crazy Henry, I was thinking of riding inside the stage, not be one of the horses pulling it."

That got a choke and laugh from a few men, which made the mayor mad. "Alright Delbert, you do what you think is best. I will send word to our county sheriff Pat Garrett."

Two days later Delbert's daughter Roberta, was on the six o'clock stage headed for Socorro with a huge note. The telegraph operator was to send it to the U.S. Marshals office in Denver, Colorado.

Another local miner had been gunned down in the street and robbed just last night. When the deputy came to investigate, twenty some odd armed outlaws confronted him and gave him one hour to get out of town or they would hunt him down and kill him.

James went for his horse and though it was dark, rode out for Lincoln. As he rode, he was mad. "Dad gum you Pat, you've gotta do something er I'm gonna quit."

He got to Lincoln just after midnight and went straight to the hotel and bed. The next morning as he ate breakfast, Roberta was well on her way to Socorro.

After his meal he walked up to Pat's office and found it closed. "Darn, I sure hope he's not off on some case."

He walked down to the livery where the hostler said, "Howdy James, come to take over for Pat?"

"Huh? Naw, just came to talk with him."

The hostler frowned, "To do that you'd have to go all the way to Las Cruces. The governor had him appointed U.S. Marshal an' that's where he went."

"Who then dad blame it is the county sheriff?"

"Nobody, all the law that's left in this county, sides our worthless local sheriff, is you an' one other deputy."

James looked at him, "No all the law left is one deputy, I quit! Tell Tim he's on his own." He got his horse and rode up to Pat's office and stuck his badge in the crack of the front door. He slowly headed back for White Oaks with a very heavy heart.

He felt he was letting the town down, but what good would it do by getting himself killed? He would ride for Fort Sumner tomorrow and leave White Oaks for good.

He made it home before dark and put his horse away. This small one room house had been his home for well over a year. He fixed himself some supper and after eating, went to packing his things.

He stopped and listened, two rifle shots came from right down town. Not thinking, out the door he ran and didn't stop until he saw a crowd of people standing around in front of the Little Casino Saloon.

He eased into the crowd and asked a fellow who was shot this time. "Two of Slaughter's men, the meanest two. Got um right in the chest. Never knowed what hit um."

"Do you know anybody that saw it when it happened?"

"Yeah, that old miner Thomas Case. Them two had drug him outside and was robbing him. This feller rode up on ah horse with ah rifle an' shot um both's what I heard. Before more of Slaughter's men came out to split what gold was got off Thomas, that feller turned that horse an' rode off behind them buildings over yonder."

"Where's Thomas now?"

"Some of his friends grabbed him up and they half ran down to the No Scum Allowed Saloon. I'd say everyone in there has a shotgun pointed right at that door."

"Anybody know what Slaughter has had to say about it?"

"Naw and who in the hell is brave enough to go in there and find out?"

"I don't know, but the fellow that did it sure as hell had better never be found. I'm gonna walk down an' see if Thomas will talk with me."

"I'd holler out before I walked in there if I's you, that er take the chance of getting shot."

James walked up the street and stood next to the door as he hollered, "James Redman comin' in!"

A voice called back, "Come ah head!"

As James walked in a man asked, "Any of Slaughter's men headed this'a way?"

"Naw, they's all in that saloon talkin'. Thomas, can you

tell me what happened?"

"Hell yeah, saved my poke an' maybe my life's what that young feller did."

"Then you saw who it was?"

"Well yeah an' no."

"Now what in the hell is that supposed to mean?"

"It was dark, he was on ah horse an' dressed in all black. He had one of them hood type things over his head an' shoulders an' ah black hat on top ah that. That little sucker jerked that horse to ah stop an' had that rifle at his shoulder in nothin' flat. He let Jess have it first an' as Hugh went fer his gun, he shot him too. That horse turned on ah dime an' he was gone 'fore one feller was out that door. At first, they didn't know what the hell happened. Yeah, then them idiots thought I'd shot um.

"I says, are you stupid? I ain't got no rifle. They turned an' hurried back inside. Then these boys grabbed me up an we hooked um fer here."

As they talked, down the street at the Little Casino, Slaughter was having a fit. "By damn it had to be that damn deputy. He get away with this it damn shor won't be the last time. I want him dead within the hour! Get damn you! Get out there an' find him!"

As four of them headed out that door, two of them were knocked back inside with one bullet each in their chest. As the sounds of those shots died away, they heard a horse running all out. Slaughter yelled, "Get the hell out there an' get him!"

Those men ran out, guns in hand but saw nothing to shoot at. That horse and rider was out of sight. They walked back in, "He's gone, never saw who it was."

"Don't be ah damn idiot! It was that deputy, nobody else would even try ah thing like that."

He got up and walked over close to the door, looking down at his men. "Damn heart shots." He walked on out front and kneeled down beside both dead men lying in the street.

He struck a match and looked at each chest. "Heart shots, all four of um. Shor wouldn't thought that deputy was that good. He didn't want um shootin' back, they's dead before they fell."

He walked back to the door and whistled, "We're ridin'!"

They went for their horses and rode from town. Belle placed her deck of cards on the table and she and bartender walked over looking at the dead men. Belle said, "I have no idea who in the hell that shooter is, but he's sure as hell hard on business. Get help and get this mess cleaned up. We still have customers to wait on."

In the No Scum Allowed Saloon, James said, "You keep sayin' young feller. Being as he was wearin' ah hood how could you tell he was young?"

"Cause he was little, yeah even littler than you. An' fast, oh yeah he was fast. Ah older feller, no way he could'a whipped that rifle up the way it was done an' shoot one an' jack ah cartridge in that firin' chamber an' get the other'n 'fore he got his gun out. Young'uns is all that can do that."

One fellow said, "Yeah, if he wadn't already dead, I'd say it was Billy the Kid."

A voice called out he was coming in. He walked in saying, "James you'd damn shor better ride. Slaughter an' his men rode out. I walked in that saloon to see what I could find out. The bartender overheard Slaughter tellin' his men it was you what shot them four men..."

"Whoa! You mean two men."

"Naw, Slaughter sent his men to get you, four of um. When they stepped out that door, two of um was shot dead. When Slaughter saw where them shots was placed, he got his men an' got the hell out'a town."

"What do you mean by placed?"

"Four dead men, four heart shots."

Thomas smiled, "Bless that feller's heart, maybe he's the archangel come to save White Oaks."

"Yeah, but I wouldn't stake my life on it. James you'd better get, Slaughter will have you killed."

"Yeah, I'm packed an' ready to ride. Pat Garrett was appointed a U.S. Marshal an' has gone over to Las Cruces. There is no longer a county sheriff. To keep from getting myself killed, I turned in my badge an' will head for Fort Sumner tomorrow."

Several men said, "Good boy, damn good thinkin. Roberta was on the mornin' stage for Socorro. She's gonna send ah wire to Denver for us ah U.S. Marshal. Just hope the hell he's better'n Pat Garrett."

A fellow said, "Now you don't know that about Pat, maybe he was sent to Las Cruces for ah reason."

"Damn shor couldn't be more important than savin' our town. Somethin' ain't done in ah hurry, we'll lose it. A town with no law don't last long out here in the west."

A man asked, "James, any idea how many different gangs hang out around here?"

"Four that I know of, might be more. Rustlers have shor killed ah few cowboys an' got ah way with gobs of cattle. Two of the mines, when they take their gold to the railroad over at Socorro, they have twenty outriders an' ah gatling gun in the back wagon. They only had to use it once is what I've heard."

"I'd say there's no gang around here big enough to try an' take it. Shor lose ah bunch ah men if they did try."

****

Over the next week, very little happened in White Oaks. Roberta had come back with an answer to that wire. A U.S. Marshal would be in White Oaks within the next week or so.

Word came that the last gold shipment headed for Socorro was held up. In a narrow canyon dynamite was thrown taking out the gatling gun first thing. Then more dynamite was used as those guards hunkered down to return fire. That day, twenty-six men were killed and over twenty thousand dollars in gold taken. Two guards that were wounded played dead. They had seen who this gang was.

"Gaylon Swayne we'll see ever damn one ah y'all dead!"

Saturday afternoon arrived and the town of White Oaks got ready for the gangs they would be riding in. Every store closed except saloons, bordellos. Men and women stayed off the street. Only cowboys and miners were in those saloons and gambling halls.

Just at sundown, gunfire erupted as two gangs rode

into town firing their guns into the air. They soon filled every saloon, except the No Scum allowed Saloon. Four armed guards with double barrel shotguns kept the peace. Two were out front sitting in chairs. Two were inside at locations they could see everyone that came thru that door, as well as everyone in that room. Gangs knew this and stayed away.

These gangs knew plenty of miners with heavy pokes would be in saloons gambling. Slaughter and his gang was in the Little Casino already raising hell.

Willie Lambert and his worthless bunch were in the Golden Spike and had already spotted their first victims. Willie smiled, "Looks like it'll be ah big payday boys. Red, you an' Bud first. Get over yonder by that back door. Outhouse time, y'all get um."

An hour later two miners got up and headed out that back door. Thirty seconds later Red and Bub stepped out and were   shot dead, one bullet in each heart. In that outhouse Gib said, "Damn Buck, that was close."

"Yeah, wonder what they's shootin at in the damn dark."

"Yeah, an' with ah damn rifle. How stupid can they be?"

They finished and headed for that back door and stopped dead still, looking at two bodies. A voice from the darkness said, "They were after you two. Get to the

No Scum and you'll be safe." They heard a horse head down the alley toward the Little Casino.

They hurried to the No Scum and Buck said, "Wonder who in the hell that was. Shor saved us ah headache an' our poke. Them looked like Willie Lambert's men."

In the Golden Spike there was so much noise, those shots wasn't heard. If they were, no one paid any attention. Buck and Gib made it to the No Scum and told everyone what happened. Several men laughed out loud with one saying, "By damn he's back. That little sucker is back! Thomas, what do you think of that?"

"I'd share my poke with him any time."

Buck asked, "You mean ever who that was done it before?"

"Shor did an' saved my hide at the same time. Jess an' Hugh had hold of me right out front of the Little Casino. That little sucker got um both in ah split second."

The owner of the saloon said, "This may be a town with no law, but somebody shor has it in for those gangs. We just have to hope the hell he's smart enough not to get caught before them U.S. Marshals get here."

Willie was wondering what the hell was keeping his men. "Cable, get the hell out there an' see what the hell they're doin! Tell um to get it done. We need them pokes."

"Yeah, but none of um's come back in, not even them miners. Think Red an' Bub would'a... Naw, I'll be right back."

And he was right back. "Willie! They're both dead!"

"Damn it they wadn't supposed to kill um. Get to that..."

"No damn it! Red an' Bub is the ones that's dead!"

CHAPTER TWO

"Two damned old miners out drawed Red an' Bub! I don't believe it! Not in ah hunnert years could they ah done that."

Out that back door he went, laying right there was both his men. He looked down saying "Jim, strike a match."

He saw that hole in both their chest and said, "Damn, heart shots." He rolled them over and saw where those slugs came out. "Wadn't them miners what shot um."

One man asked, "How'n the hell do you know that?"

"That was a rifle what got um, bullets went all the way thru. Pistol wouldn't blowed a hole that big an' shor's hell wouldn'a gone plumb thru um. Look where they came out. Looks like we have us ah shooter… Whoa now, maybe that little deputy growed some balls after all. Maybe we ought'a just look him up."

Another man said, "By damn I'm fer that 'fore he gets any more of us."

They all walked back in and sat for a drink. "Buford, think you an' Carlie can handle him er do you need more help?"

"You know better'n that! I'd bet that little snot is at that office laughin' his butt off. We'll get him an' be back."

They walked out that front door and were slammed back thru that door, dead. Those rifle shots were heard loud and clear this time and every man in there hit the floor, guns in hand. On his knees, Willie hollered, "Somebody blow out that damn…" A bullet hit him right between the eyes. Pistol shots quickly blew out those lamps and everyone lay very still and quiet, guns pointed toward that front door.

It was so quiet in there when a man farted, every ear in the place heard it and at the same time a horse was heard running up the street. One man hollered "Let's get him!"

Another said, "Stay down you stupid…! You don't know that was his horse!"

It was dark in there and it was over fifteen minutes before the bartender started lighting lamps. Men all around the room slowly got off the floor and sat in their chairs. A miner looked down at Willie and said, "Damn, blowed the back of his head out. Wonder what kind'a bullets that feller is usin."

Willie's men eased out that door and grabbed horses from the hitch rail. They headed toward Lincoln, but just rode to the creek and stopped for the night. One asked, "What er we gonna do without Willie."

Another said, "Hell, just join up with us some more boys… Wait just ah damn minute! Damn I most forgot! I know where Willie's stash was kept back there in that house!"

Horses were mounted and it was an all-out horse race back to the house where that gang had been staying. As soon as they walked thru the door, they were striking matches to light the lamps. Roman, with a lamp in his left hand headed to the fireplace and reached back behind, pulling out a loose rock. He dropped it to the floor and reached in that hole. Smiling he tugged and tugged and pulled out a huge leather pouch.

"Here it is boys! By damn here it is!"

He set the lamp on the table then emptied that bag right in the middle. Paper money, gold and silver coins and nuggets spilled everywhere. "Look at that! That dirty skunk was holdin' out on us! Yeah, an' he said he was nigh on to broke." They were all sitting, bug eyed.

"Just in case we have to split up, we'll count all this out right now dollar fer dollar fer each of us 'cept them nuggets. We'll look at the size of them first."

With no arguing, it took over two hours dividing up Willie's money. Before leaning back, one of them walked to a cabinet and pulled out a bottle of whiskey.

As they sat there drinking at their good luck of Willie getting killed, one of them took the glass away from his lips and said, "By damn I wonder who in the hell it was that upped an' killed Jess an' Hugh then got Carlie an'

Buford. Ever who it was is damn good gettin' Willie thru that winder. All of um with ah rifle."

They all sat there not saying a word for five minutes. After a bit one said, "That was five of us what was got tonight. You boys thinkin' maybe some miner just got enough of us an's gonna wipe us all out?"

"Could by damn, but not if we ride out'a here come mornin'. We could go over to Chloride er Hillsboro. Them's silver minin' towns."

Rob had been sitting there not saying a word. He was the oldest of the bunch. Roman asked, "What cha got on yore mind, Rob?"

"Mexico. With what I've got right here I'm gettin' the hell clean out'a this territory. Somebody has it in fer us an' might not quit 'til they get us all."

Another said, "I don't give ah damn where we go as long as we go. We'll have coffee an' breakfast here in the mornin' an' not go into town fer nothin. We'll split all this grub we can carry between us an' coffee an' ride like hell."

****

The next morning as they rode out, those two wounded guards that lived thru the gold robbery were back with a dozen men and three wagons. They were picking up the dead, taking them into Socorro to be buried.

One of those men said, "Looks as if a different route will have to be taken for gold shipments from now on. Any shipment could be hit right here in this narrow canyon."

One of those guards said, "One thing, I find um this bunch won't be robbin' no more. They won't remember me, but I'll get ever damn one of um if it takes ah year."

Gaylon and those men were on their way to White Oaks, camped just a few miles west. As they sat drinking morning coffee, one of those men asked, "How er we gonna get rid of this all this gold an' turn it into spendin' money?"

"A dab at ah time. Gamble, buy somethin' and get paper money in change. We'll go out an' see if Willie will let us stay with him an' his bunch in that big ol' house. Hell, we could stay in that barn if we had to. It's big enough."

Another said, "Hell with this kind'a money I'd like to stay in one of them hotels. You know, close to all them bordellos an' women an' gamblin' halls."

Gaylon said, "Some of us just might do that, later. Now I want not one word spread around where it's knowed what we done. Not even Willie's bunch is to know."

Pete said, "Yeah but it's ah shame we can't rub it in Jack Slaughter's face. He was always sayin' he'd not try them shipments after that gattlin' gun was used on Howler's bunch. Got um ever damn one, horses too."

Gaylon laughed, "Yeah but as you boys know, Howler nor Jack never was as smart as me. I figger things out first."

Two and a half hours later they rode up to Willie's place. "Damn, this early an' they're already gone. We'll take care of the horses anyhow an' hang ah round 'til they get back. Broke as he always is he might want us to pay."

Pete said, "I'd damn shor rather stay in a hotel."

"You said that, Pete! We can't go in there carryin' these bags of gold."

"Then by damn 'fore Willie an' nem get back, why don't we find us ah good buryin' place fer most of it. We could go on into town an' get us ah woman."

Gaylon said, "Now that's ah hell of ah idea. Boys get to lookin' fer the best place where Willie an' his boys won't stumble onto it."

"How ah bout we get ah shovel an bury it in that back stall? Right against the wall in one corner ought'a do er. Deep ah nuff an' cover it with horseshit where nobody'd ever find it."

"Then get to digin' we don't know when they'll be back. I'm goin' on in an' get coffee water on. Oh, everybody keep out about ah hundred-dollars in nuggets, no gold bars."

They headed for the barn and Gaylon walked into the house. He looked around sayin' "Damn, they're nigh plumb out'a grub an' I see no coffee." He walked out to his horse and reached in his saddlebags for a sack of coffee.

He got half way upon the porch and looked back at his horse. Smiling, he walked back and got a bottle of whiskey. "Just ah dab of whiskey always goes good with coffee."

They hung around until around four and Gaylon said, "Let's get on into town. Willie an' nem must be off on ah job."

Snowball asked, "We goin to Belle La Mar's?"

"We are, now if Slaughter's bunch is in there, keep yer mouths shut."

"I thought we'd go to the Golden Spike an' look up Willie an' nem."

"We'll do that later, cause Belle La Mar has bigger poker games an' I want'a win me some money. I feel lucky."

Two men laughed with one saying, "Yeah, ol' Varnish Belle will clean yore plow. She's slicker than hog snot on ah door knob."

As they rode in, a fellow looked over at Snowball. "Snowball, you never told us, was you born with that white hair? Hell, you can't be more'n thirty,"

Snowball grinned, "Naw, back when I's around twenty er so, I was stretched out sound ah sleep. I felt ah hot breath on my face an' opened my eyes. Starin' me eyeball to eyeball was ah mountain lion. I squirted tobacco juice in one of his eyes. Made him madder'n hell. He growled, so I growled back fer maybe as long at three er four minutes we growled. I was so damn scared I shit my pants. That sucker smelled it, shook his head an' turned an' run.

"When I got back to the ranch, one of the boys looked at me with his mouth open. He says, Freddy, what in the hell happened to you?"

"I says, what do you mean? He told me my hair was snow white. I looked in ah mirror an' shor nuff it was white. Everybody got to callin' me Snowball an' it stuck."

"I don't believe ah damn word ah that!"

"Go to hell Colder! That's what happened."

Gaylon hollered, "Y'all just shut the hell up! Colder, you

asked, he told! Now that's ah bout ah nuff."

Thirty minutes later they were in the Little Casino, looking all around. Gaylon said, "Don't see Jack an' his bunch. Guess they went off on ah nother job."

Belle's table was full of gamblers, so Gaylon walked over to another. Four of the men grabbed women and walked off down the hallway. The other three got a bottle and sat at a table talking.

They had been sitting there and it was now after dark. All of a sudden, they heard two rifle shots so close together they almost sounded as one. The whole place went quiet. After several minutes Belle said, "Those shots came from up around the Opera House Saloon. I wonder who that little skunk got this time."

Gaylon laid his cards face down and walked over close to her. "You got some idea what them shots was?"

"I do, pistol shots I pay no mind. Rifle shots mean more men just died."

"What in the hell are you talkin' about?"

"Oh yeah, you boys have been gone for over a week. Maybe you're the lucky ones."

"Belle! Damn it you ain't makin' no sense."

She grinned, "For starters, four of Jack's men was killed right here, two on the way to the outhouse an' two at the front door. A few nights later down at the Golden Spike, Jess and Hugh were shot out back and Red and Bub at the front door. Everyone was hunkered down and a bullet came thru the front window and got Willie smack dab between the eyes. The rest of Willie's men haven't been seen since. Now two more rifle shots, I'll lay odds two more men are dead."

"Damn! Willie's dead! You think maybe that little deputy is doin' it?"

"Naw, he quit and left town. White Oaks is a town with no law. Well, maybe vigilante law. That sometimes works better than real law."

"Yeah, but nobody knows who's shooting at um."

"Nope, I'd say it's a miner somebody robbed and let live. Some of those old boys can be tougher that saddle leather."

As they talked, two men came in. One asked, "Y'all hear ah bout that shootin' done in front of the Opera House?"

"Naw, heard the shots is all."

"Ah couple of Billy Hart's men caught ah rifle bullet right smack dab in the heart. Guess they won't be slappin' no more girls ah round."

"Anybody see who done it?"

"It was said it was just ah kid on ah horse. Wears ah black type hood an' robe, covers his whole body. Black hat an' all. Wilford even said he thinks he saw he was wearin' black gloves. Fast horse is what was said. He was gone time them ol' boys hit the ground."

Gaylon asked Belle, "Have you seen Jack lately?"

"Yes, he said he wouldn't be in tonight until around nine. Give him another hour."

Gaylon walked back to the table he was playing cards at and pitched in his hand then picked up his money. "That's all fer me." He moved over to the table where three of his men were.

"Boys, looks like maybe a problem here in White Oaks. You heard what Belle said. Not countin' how many was shot tonight, nine er so's already been shot dead."

"Yeah, but nobody but law would be after us. I'd say we don't got no worry."

"Hope the hell yer right. Course we ain't thumped no miner anywhere close to here. Belle thinks it could be ah mad miner."

"I thought that feller said it was ah kid."

"Now how in the hell would he know that if he had on ah hood an' black robe? It could be ah really little miner."

A half hour or so later, in walked Jack Slaughter and his men. Gaylon called them over, having his men move to the next table. Jack walked over and looked at him. "Yeah?"

"I'll get us ah bottle, maybe we ought'a do some talkin' an' rackin' our brains."

"Been doin' ah hell of ah lot of that these past few days." He took a chair and Gaylon waved to the bartender for a bottle and glasses.

The bottle was brought and drinks were poured. Gaylon said, "With White Oaks being a town with no law… Hell, this whole county don't got no law. Pat Garrett went to Las Cruces. Anyhow what do you think of us all just go to killin' ever miner we see?"

"Are out of yore damn mind? That's where me an' my boys get our money an' gold. That's why we hadn't killed no more of um than we just had to. Naw, get that out'a yore head."

"That's up to you, but you've already lost four men an' Willie's dead and what was left of his gang, they run."

They both took glasses to their mouths and had a long drink. Jack said, "Now maybe, you might'a hit on somethin' there. What if we just killed ever little bitty miner we see. Ever body that's saw him said it was ah little kid. We know damn good'n well no kid would do that. It had to be ah really little miner that we roughed up an' robbed."

"Yeah, we'll just take our time an' get it done. We'll have to let the men know only little fellers is to be killed. Hell, there can't be more'n ah half dozen of um."

"Not tonight though, we have drinkin' an' women to visit"

"To beat that, with no law broad daylight would be best."

"Yeah, that'd be best so the men can see how big they really are. I have to look at it this'a way, ever miner we kill could be takin' money out'a my pocket. We have to tell the men not to go hog wild an' just go to shootin'."

"When you want'a start?"

"Late tomorrow afternoon. Miners most times don't get to town 'til late."

"Yeah, hell me an' the boys won't be up 'til noon anyhow."

****

The next day just before noon, Blum and Ted, two of Billy's heart's men walked into the grocery store. Several women and girls were in there buying their groceries. Blum walked over to pick up a sack of coffee and knocked Mrs. Denton to the floor, because he thought she was in his way.

Mister Twain ran over picking her up. "Fellow, there was no call for that! Get out, now!"

"Go to hell, I ain't got all I want yet."

He started to push Blum, before he could Ted knocked him flat. "We ain't done, Feller!"

The other women and girls fled the store as Mrs. Twain helped Mrs. Denton to a chair, then ran and kneeled down beside her husband. She ran to the back for water and a rag, as Blum and Ted were helping themselves to whatever they wanted. With arms full they walked out without paying.

Mister Twain came to and sat up. The first thing he asked was, "How is Kathy?"

"She'll be fine, a little shaken is all. How do you feel?"

"He sure rattled my brain there for a minute, I'll be alright. What did they walk out with?"

"I didn't see it all but coffee, flour and jerky. Oh, and a

gallon of Karo Syrup."

"The next time those men walk in, I'll pull that shotgun from under the counter. Billy Hart will pay for that or I will have them all arrested."

Mrs. Denton said, "Albert, White Oaks is a town with no law."

"I forgot that for the moment. Dear, you watch things I'm going straight to the mayor. If he doesn't hire us a sheriff, I'll send off for a paid gun hand... But wait, there's supposed to be a U.S. Marshal on his way. Do you remember when Roberta said he would be here?"

"No, but anytime now I would think."

Those women and girls that ran from the store, very quickly spread the news of what had gone on in the grocery store and told it was Blum and Ted, two of Billy Hart's men.

That night when Billy and his men settled in for a night of drinking and poker in the Opera Saloon, they were in for a surprise. Right a nine o'clock sharp, a hooded rider showed up right outside. The window was peeked thru, then the horse was remounted.

The horse was moved two feet farther west so Blum and Ted could plainly be seen thru the window sitting at that card table. Through that window, two rifle shots so close together no one had time to react as Ted and Blum were knocked over backwards with a bullet in each of their hearts.

Before men got their thoughts about them, they heard a horse being run down the street. Billy and the rest of his men were out that door firing blindly into the dark night. That horse had been turned right at the first street. Those bullets hit nothing but air. That shooter was sure bullets would fly and had the escape route already picked out well in advance. Tomorrow there just might be a few more dead outlaws in White Oaks.

The rider went on home, unsaddled the horse and clothes were changed in the barn and hidden. No one must not know what was done until they hear about it tomorrow. Anyone find out, their lives could be in danger until not one outlaw was left to do harm to the people of White Oaks.

The next day just before noon, a young cowboy was seen riding toward the livery on a beautiful dun stud. Girls, even women smiled when he looked their way. A teen age girl said, "Dead Lord, I pray he's not an outlaw, he's so cute."

Her mother gasp for breath. "Twana June! What are you saying?"

"I'm saying I hope he's not an outlaw and stays around White Oaks."

"Well, I never…" Twana June's mother smiled, "Yes, that might be nice to have a nice clean-cut boy around."

"Mama, he wasn't a boy, he is a grown man."

"To me he's just a boy, Dear."

Shorty rode up to the livery and the hostler said howdy. "You be leavin' that dun?"

"Yes Sir, shor will. Can you tell me where I would find a feller named Delbert Masters?"

"Could, anything important?"

"He said it was."

The hostler pointed, "Take that street right there an' go past the grave yard. His is the third house on the left."

"Then I'd best hold off on stallin' my horse 'til I get back."

Shorty rode up in front of a house with a picket fence and dismounted. Walking up the walkway, a pretty girl walked out the front door and stopped. "Hello, are you looking for my dad?"

"I am if he's Delbert Masters."

"He is and I'm Roberta."

"Howdy Roberta, I'm U.S. Marshal Shorty Thompson."

"What took you so long getting here?"

"Oh, being as I only had a little over two hundred miles to ride, I stopped off and fished along the way then went hunting for a few days. I laid up drunk back in…"

She laughed, "I'll get dad."

Shorty and Delbert talked, with Delbert telling everything that had been goin go. "Now Marshal…"

"Hold it, until I get a handle on this, nobody is to know I'm ah marshal. I want to live long enough to do some good."

Delbert looked at his daughter, "Did you hear that, Roberta? Don't be spreading it around he's here."

"Shorty, we have no law at all in White Oaks being as Pat Garrett left and his deputy that was assigned to White Oaks quit and left town. That was to save his own life, he had been threatened."

"I'd say he was pretty smart. Now I'm sure most folks know most of the gangs, I don't so this is going to take me a few days. Is there a jail?"

"There is, it only has two big cells as all prisoners, if it was a serious crime was taken over to Lincoln."

"What about yore mayor's mouth? Should I let him know I'm here?"

"I wouldn't just now. He can't keep his mouth shut, brags."

CHAPTER THREE

Shorty told them for the time being he was just a little cowboy that came to town for a while. "One more thing Shorty, since the wire we sent you over a dozen outlaws have been shot dead around saloons."

"Dad gum, are gangs killin' each other off?"

"No, every man except one has been shot dead center of the heart. Willie Lambert, the leader of one of the gangs was shot between the eyes. Everyone of them was shot with a rifle. The fellow that is doing it wears a black hood and robe. I'm sure that is so he won't be recognized. Word is about the outlaws thinks it's a very small miner. Everyone else thinks it's a young boy because the men that have seen him says he very small and is very fast with that rifle."

"Not good, I'm new in town. I just hope ever who it is don't think I'm an outlaw."

"To date, every one of them that has shot was trying to rob a miner or had slapped women around."

"I won't be doin' any of that so maybe I'll be safe. Remember, you see me around you don't know me. I'm sure everyone knows you sent for a marshal."

"How did you find where I live?"

"Asked the hostler."

"When you go to stall your horse, you'd better make up a story of why you were looking for me. Inadvertently he will spread it around a marshal is in town. One more thing, the only safe saloon in town for locals and cowboys is the No Scum Aloud. Gangs have taken over every other one."

"Sooner er later them is the ones I'll have to go in. I have to see and get to know what each outlaw looks like. I'll try to keep my nose real short an' not ask to many questions."

As he rode back to the livery, the Slaughter and Swayne gangs were in the Little Casino having their first drink of the afternoon. "Gaylon to keep from killin' off too many miners, I've told my men to only kill little ones that's carryin' ah rifle. I'd like it if you'd tell yore men the same."

"Oh yeah, that'd be best to start off with. The fewer we have to kill, the more you'll be able to rob later on. How about we go ah head an' kill any little feller we see with ah rifle, miner er not? You know some of them cowboys are mighty handy with ah rifle."

"Yeah, that's ah good idea. One more thing, we only send ah couple men out on the street at one time. That'a way it won't scare folks onto hidin'."

"Yeah, one ah my men'll go with one of yours. When do you think we ought'a send the first two?"

"Anytime now, them miners ought'a be showin' up.

Shorty was stalling Dunnie and the hostler asked, "What'd Delbert have to say?"

"Said he wadn't interested."

"Interested in what?"

"Goin' in partners with me in ah gold mine."

"Ah gold mine! You got ah gold mine!"

"Not yet but I might stumble on one 'fore too long."

Shorty took his saddlebags and threw them over his left shoulder, then picked up his rifle with his left hand. The hostler asked, "You gonna stay ah round?"

"Might fer ah couple weeks er so, just 'til I find that gold mine. I shor do need one."

"Son them mountains has been crawled over by the best ol' timers in the west. There ain't none that hadn't already been found, mark my words."

"Yeah, but I've gotta see that for myself. That dun horse of mine can smell an' spot gold a hundred yards away."

"The hell you say!"

"Fer ah fact. I'll be back in the mornin'."

Almost at that same time, Jack and Gaylon sent two men, Harold and Goober to find little men with rifles and kill them. A good block or better before Shorty got to the hotel, Goober said, "Harold, yonder comes one now. You want him er do I take him?"

"Go ah head, you saw him first."

Goober pulled his pistol and as it was brought up almost level, he was knocked flat of his back with a bullet in his heart. Harold grabbed for his pistol and Shorty shot him dead. Looking behind him, he saw as a hooded, robed rider cut a horse off the street and was out of sight.

If not for that rider, surely Shorty would have taken a bullet, he hadn't even seen what those two men were up to. Two business men stepped from the shops saying, "Good shooting Cowboy! You got both of them. That one there on his back is Goober, he rides with the Jack Slaughter gang. The one on his side is Harold, rides with Gaylon Swayne."

"Don't know um, never saw um before so why was they gunnin' for me?"

"I'd say they saw the hooded rider behind you and was

going for him."

"Might'a been, his rifle shot got that'n there. When the other'n went for his gun, I got him. Y'all will have to get the undertaker, I'm new in town an' don't know where he's at."

Shorty went on toward the hotel but stopped and turned, looking the way that rider had gone. He got his room then walked all the way to the No Scum Allowed Saloon. The only thing everyone was talking about was the hooded rider got two more men.

One fellow said, "It'll take him time, but he shor is whittlin' um down a couple at a time."

It was almost an hour before Jack said, "I can't believe it's takin' Goober an' Harold this long to find ah miner er two."

He hollered over to one of his men, "Len, go find out what the hell's keepin' um."

Len, as he got up laughed, "Maybe they got ah couple ol' boys that had big pokes on um an' hooked um."

Jack said, "They'd damn shor better not run off with my gold! They know better'n that."

Gaylon said, "Naw, Harold wouldn't ah done that."

It was well over thirty minutes before Len came walkin' back in. Before he said one word, Jack said, "You mean you didn't find um! Go to ever damn saloon..."

"Oh, but I found um alright. Both of um's over at the undertaker's office. That undertaker said one of um was got with a rifle bullet to the heart, the other'n was got with ah pistol shot to the head. They's both deader'n hell alright."

Gaylon and Jack sat there looking at each other. Gaylon got up and went to the bar and got four bottles of whiskey. Turning he hollered to his men, "Let's ride boys! This town with no law is gettin' a dab dangerous. We'll come back after it settles down some."

Jack stood, "Where are you boys headed? We could sit right here an' get um all when they come thru that door."

"Naw, we'll leave that up to you. Being as Willie's dead an' his boys rode out an' we went an' took over his place."

"By damn that was ah good idea an' ain't all that far. Me an' my boys are gonna hang ah round an' see how many of them miners are brave enough to stick their heads thru that door. Might just get ah few of um."

Gaylon and his men walked out and mounted their horses. As they turned down the street headed southwest two rifle shots rang out. Two of his men were knocked from their saddles with bullets in their chest.

Gaylon and the other men laid low over those saddle horns and rode with all the speed they could get out of their horses.

When they were out of range of any rifle, they slowed and Gaylon asked, "Who got it?"

One of the men said, "Demy an' Coleman. They was on each side of me. Damn it one of them shots could'a got me."

Gaylon laughed, "Don't be sacred Floyd, you just got richer with them three dead."

"Damn you Gaylon! That ain't funny by damn."

"Wadn't meant to be. We've got whiskey an' coffee. Runnin' low on grub but one of us will go back to town real early some mornin' an' get more. No shooter ought'a be out that early. Oh, an' the grub is to be paid for."

Another man asked, "What er we gonna do if Jack er Billy's men don't find who's killin' ever body?"

"I'd say we stay the hell out'a White Oaks for ah spell."

"Yeah, Gaylon, with the gold an' money we've got right now we could ride the hell out'a this country just like Willie's boys done. I'm not too damn proud to run when it could mean my life to stay."

"Hold on, damn it just hold on! If we have to ride, I'll be the one that says when. I'd like to find out when another big gold shipment is gonna take place an' us hit it. Then by damn we run. Another twenty to fifty thousand dollars, I want. By damn you just name me any other town with no law. So, we have one shooter, that beats the hell out of ah sheriff an' ah few deputies."

Curly said, "I'm not goin' to town. I'll stay right here."

"You'll do by damn what I say er ride! Now get them horses took care of. I'll get on inside an' get lamps lit, keepin' company with one ah these bottles."

****

Shorty was in the No Scum Allowed Saloon drinking a beer and listening to as many conversations as he could. Most of the talk was about a young hooded rider that was doing something about the outlaw element in White Oaks. Something the law seemed unable to do, kill them.

Shorty was sitting at a table close to two elderly miners. He said, "Looks like somebody would know who he is."

One of those miners looked over at him. "Cowboy, we damn shor don't need to know who he is as long as he keeps doin' what he's doin'. I ain't never felt safe in this town 'til now. Our only worry is when we leave ah saloon after dark. That boy can't be ever where at once."

"Yeah, even though he saved my hide a bit ah go, what if he ups an' shoots the wrong man someday?"

"Ain't happened yet an' bet it don't. He knows ever one of um. It seems the ones that don't pull no crap here in town's left ah lone. Mess with ah miner er somebody in ah store, they've damn shor got their selves ah problem. If Pat Garrett had ah been the County Sheriff he's supposed to ah been, this would'a never got out'a hand to start with. We've lost ah lot'a good friends an' more gold than you'd ever know. None of us carries ah poke of any size no more."

Shorty listened some more but knew good and well tomorrow night he would have to visit one of the other saloons. He had to see every outlaw and remember his face if he was going to get them one or two at a time. He sure as hell didn't want to get into a gunfight with more than one or two at a time.

The next evening after an early supper, Shorty walked into the Golden Spike Saloon. Standing at the end of the bar, he called for a beer. Billy Hart and his men noticed him at once. Billy asked, "Any of you boys seen that cowboy before?"

They all said no and one said, "I wouldn't think he's the shooter, he's new around here."

"If he gets nosy, we'll find out what he's up to."

"He wouldn't be dumb enough to cause trouble in here."

Another one said, "Yeah, an' he don't got no rifle with him."

"He wouldn't brought it in here with him anyhow. Go out an' see if he has one on his saddle."

"How'll I know what horse he's ridin'?"

"Any horses out there but ours with rifles on um, come back in an' ask which horse is his."

Dean was back in a couple minutes and stopped, looking at Shorty. "Say Cowboy, which one of them horses are you ridin'?"

Shorty looked at him, "I'm not ridin' at all, I'm standin' here drinkin' ah beer."

"Yer smart, huh?"

Shorty never batted an eye as he said, "Yer dumb, huh?"

The fellow backed up, lowering his hand to his gun butt. "You lookin' fer trouble Cowboy?"

"Naw not really, why?"

"Well by damn if you did, you came to the right place!"

"Why don't you go pester somebody else while I drink my beer? You leave me alone, I'll damn shor leave you alone. Why would you want to take the chance of gettin' shot cause it's none of yore damn business which horse might be mine."

"Well, I... You own ah rifle?"

"Do you know of one cowboy that don't? Hell yes, I own ah rifle an' damn shor know how to use it."

The fellow saw this cowboy wasn't intimidated and sure wasn't backing down. He looked back at Billy, not knowing what to do. Billy said, "Neil, get over there an' see what the hell's wrong with Dean. He ought'a already slapped that little cowboy plumb stupid. He wadn't supposed to take no lip."

Neil swaggered over there asking, "This little runt givin' you trouble, Dean?"

"Naw I... Well yeah, he won't tell me which horse is his but did say he owns ah rifle."

"Then by damn maybe he'll tell me! Won't you Cowboy!"

"Naw, like I told him, it's none ah yore damn business."

"What if I want to make it my business?"

"Bigger men than you're tried."

"Wye you little…" He drew back and swung a blow, but Shorty quickly jerked Dean right between them.

Dean was hit in the left temple and went all the way down to one knee. He shook his head and got up. "Ought'a not done that Neil." He knocked the hell out of him, sending him flat of his back and under a table.

Billy yelled, "What in the hell are y'all doin'?"

Dean looked at him and said, "By damn he hit me first! You know nobody hits me."

Shorty finished his beer saying, "I see you boys have something to talk about, it's my bed time." He walked out.

Billy walked over, "I sent y'all to find out what the hell that cowboy was doin' in here! I damn shor didn't say try to kill each other."

"Then by damn you tell Neil he don't got to hit me. You know that makes me mad. I's doin' what you told me to do."

"Pour water on him an' bring him to then sit yore butts down!"

By the time Neil came to, Dean was back at the table

with a drink in his hand. Neil leaned over the table getting right in his face. "What'n the hell did you do that for?"

"By damn you hit me?"

"Idiot! You stupid idiot! I wouldn't have if you hadn't stepped in front of that blow. It was meant for…"

Dean, with both hands flat on the table said, "Idiot! You callin' me ah idiot!" From a sitting position, he swung a right that knocked Neil on his back, out cold.

He looked at Billy, "You know nobody hits me er calls me ah idiot."

"Yeah, I knowed it, guess Neil does now."

One man asked, "Billy, you thinkin' maybe we ought'a ride 'til that shooter stops. I'd hate to catch ah bullet."

"Might, later. If there ain't too many gangs over around Chloride, Winston er Hillsboro we might could do some good. Maybe Slaughter an' Swayne's bunch can smoke this sucker out an' kill him. They said they's gonna start shootin' every little miner an' cowboy they see with ah rifle."

"What about that little cowboy what was just here?"

"Naw, if it was him, he shor's hell wouldn'a walked in

here an' took the chance of gettin' shot."

Dean said, "I can't believe it, here we have ah town with no law an' have lost more men than ever before."

"Like Slaughter said, we've made some miner madder'n hell an' he's out to get even."

"By damn he's got more'n even already."

Another said, "Think we ought'a go to payin' fer stuff."

"Like what stuff?"

"Ever damn thing we get, food, bullets, boots, clothes an', well you know, ever thing."

"Are you out'a yore damn mind! You start that we'd have to keep it up. Hell no, we ain't payin' fer nothin'."

****

At last, the two guards that lived thru that robbery were back at the mine office and told of the robbery and the men being killed. Ray said, "Mister Baxter, me an' Gerald are goin' after that gang. We saw ever one of um, we'll start in White Oaks, being as that's the closest town."

"No, neither of you are any shape to hunt men. I don't want you men doing that, we'll get the law on to it."

"Mister Baxter, maybe I didn't make myself clear. We wadn't askin', we was tellin'. Everyone of those men killed were friends of ours, yes family men. We will make it right."

"Now hold on Ray, give me time to put a reward out and send for U.S. Marshals. I'll offer ten per-cent of every dime that is recovered."

"Mister Baxter, Sir, we don't give a damn about your gold. We are going to kill outlaws. If it so happens, we do get any gold back, we will bring it to you. You can get whatever law you can, meantime we'll do some killin' of our own."

All the next day Ray and Gerald cleaned every rifle and pistol they had. They checked their cartridge supply and Ray said, "First thing when we get to town, we'll stop by that new gun shop and stock up. Gerald, you know if we don't find um there, we'll have to head over to Socorro."

"Ray, you know I'd go within two miles of hell to kill um all. We'll ride come early morning."

The Swayne and Slaughter gangs were at Willie's old hideout, drinking and planning. Jack said, "We're still gonna have to kill ever little miner we see. No since on us takin' any more chances of losin' more men."

"Yeah, we get rid of ever who's doin' it, that town'll be wide open being as there's no law."

"I think we ought'a send in ah couple men late this evening. Might be able to pick up ah couple good size pokes."

"Hell of ah idea, want'a ask who wants to go er just go ah ahead an' send um?"

"We can ask, nobody want'a go then we tell um."

Jack called over to the men. "Hey Sully you want'a get somebody to ride with you an' y'all go in an' see how many pokes you can get tonight? Might could be a big un."

"Hell yeah! Beat's sittin' ah round here doin' nothin."

He spoke to the fellow sitting next to him. "How about it, Ned, you too chicken er are you goin' with me."

"I'm goin' but I'm gonna get me ah woman first off then we'll get us ah couple miners."

Gaylon said, "Go ah head but by damn don't forget what you went in for."

As they were riding in, two of Billy's men were in the mercantile looking for another coffee pot. One of their men had been cleaning his gun and blew a hole in the one that had. Billy and the rest of his men were in the Golden Spike raising hell as usual.

At the Golden Spike, a miner had enough and told the bartender until he got rid of all the trash, he'd not be back. "There's four other saloons in this town you know."

That miner was a half block from the No Scum Allowed Saloon when Sully and Ned came riding in. "Would you just looky there, Sully! We've got us one already!"

They kicked their horses and cut him off. Any way he turned a horse blocked him. "Old man just hand over yore poke an' we won't have to put ah bullet in you an' take it off yore body."

The old man reached in his pocket and pulled out a small pouch. "This is the third time y'all skunks have robbed..."

Before he could hand it up to them, both were shot dead with a bullet in their hearts. They fell to the street with a thud. That old man, it scared the hell out of him and he turned to run and saw a hooded rider turn a horse off the street.

"Be damn! He got two more of um!"

As fast as those old legs could carry him, he ran into the No Scum Allowed Saloon. He hollered, "I was bein' robbed an' by damn the hooded rider got um both! Gimme ah drink, I damn near wet my pants when them two fellers hit that street deader than ah stomped on

Bull Frog."

Shorty asked, "You ever see um before?"

"Yeah, one of um was along when I was robbed twice before. I think, if I memmer right, he rides with Jack Slaughter. Don't memmer ever seein' the other'n."

Shorty asked where that was, then got up and walked down the street just as the mercantile owner ran out in the street. "Stop those men! They just robber me!

They both turned and shot at him but missed as he ducked back inside. They laughed and walked on. Shorty stood from looking at those two bodies and knocked the hell out of one of those men then shot the other one as he started bringing up his pistol.

"Get the hell up, you ain't dead. Now both of y'all hand me that money you just took from the mercantile."

"Cowboy you just dug yore own grave! You won't get to spend one dime of it! You got any idea who we ride with?"

"Naw, why don't you tell me?"

"Billy Hart an' he'll kill you for what you just went an' done. Nobody robs two of Billy's men an' lives very long."

"That money, now!"

They handed him the money and he said, "That ain't enough, empty yore pockets an' you hold out on me I blow off a knee cap."

"You can't rob…"

Shorty cocked that pistol and pointed it at a knee. "Hold it! Damn it hold it!" They emptied their pockets and there was a tidy sum.

Shorty smiled, "You fellers have no idea how much I thank you. I was getting' ah dab low on money. Now beat it while I'm in ah good mood."

The one that wasn't shot helped the other one down the street and Shorty watched as they went into the Golden Spike Saloon. Shorty walked over to the mercantile and handed him a fist full of money.

"My goodness! This is ten times what was taken!"

"They felt so bad about what they did, they wanted you to have it all."

"Cowboy, I think you are definitely pulling my leg."

"Maybe a dab, that just pays for some of the things they've took from you an' didn't pay."

"This will sure help along those lines, thanks."

Billy's two boys were talking with Billy. "You memmer that little cowboy what came in here the other night an' Neil an' Dean went over to give him some lip?"

"Well yeah, they got in a damn fight instead. What about him?"

"He just robbed us."

"He what?"

"Yeah, shor's hell did. We just took some stuff from the hardware an' emptied his cashbox an... Oh, somebody just went an' shot Sully an' Ned, killed um both."

"Was it that cowboy?"

"Naw, he didn't have no rifle an' they had holes blowed plumb thru um."

"But he robbed y'all."

"Yeah, an' not only took the mercantile's money, but made us empty our pockets an' took all of ours."

"Now if that ain't a gutsy little... I'm gonna have to have ah talk with that boy, yeah, 'fore I kill him."

He looked at one and said, "Damn Corker, yer bleedin' all over the place, what happened?"

"That cowboy shot me in my gun hand."

"That does it, he's dead! Where'd he go?"

"Didn't see. He told us to get while he was still in ah good mood. He coulda killed us you know."

CHAPTER FOUR

The next morning as Ray and Gerald rode into town, Roberta was on her way over to see Wanda Jorden. They hadn't seen each other in weeks.

As she rode up, she saw Wanda giving her horse a rub down. Wanda looked up, "Hi Roberta."

Roberta stepped from her saddle and patted Wanda's black horse on the shoulder. "You sure keep that coat shining. I haven't seen you in town as of late and rode out to make sure you're alright."

"Yes, I'm fine. I just don't go to town any more unless it's with Dad. Although we all go to church every Sunday. I haven't seen you there in the last couple of weeks. Those men scared the living tar out of me. I don't think the mayor is going to pay a sheriff enough, so he'll never get one hired."

"I know a U.S. Marshal is coming. Perhaps he will be able to do something about those gangs. Has your dad told you several more of those outlaws have been shot right on the street?"

"My goodness no! Does anyone have an idea who is doing it?"

"Not in the slightest. Those men are just shot and the rider disappears. I don't think anyone really wants to find out, they are afraid it would only bring trouble for the both of them."

"Any idea when a marshal will show up?"

"Anytime now I'm thinking." Roberta really did want to tell her best friend Shorty in already here, but she promised."

Wanda looked at her. "I wonder what that marshal would do if he ever found out who the shooter is."

"Nothing I wouldn't think. He's just doing what the law couldn't or wouldn't. Oh, I heard a young cowboy has gotten a couple of them and that hooded rider even saved him from being shot."

"Yes, I just hope that cowboy doesn't interfere."

"Interfere? I don't understand?"

"You know, with the shooter."

"Oh, I'm sure he'd not do that. I think he's going to help the shooter."

As they talked, Ray and Gerald dismounted and tied their horses in front of the gun shop. ".44's an' .44-70's, four boxes of each."

The store owner said, "Ray, looks as if both of y'all have

had ah close call."

"Yeah, that last shipment was robbed an' everybody killed 'cept us two."

"Good Heavens! When will all of this stop?"

Gerald said, "When folks has had enough and take up guns. Them outlaws have by damn killed enough of us. It's our turn now."

"You're not thinking of…"

"We shor's hell are! We saw ever one of um. When we see them, we'll bide our time an' get um one er two at a time. Just you keep yore mouth shut. Word get ah round it shor would hurt."

"I'd say you have to be careful where that hooded shooter doesn't think you two are outlaws. Him and a little cowboy sure has taken out a gob of them"

****

Out at Willie's old place the Slaughter and Swayne bunch were just now getting up and sitting around waiting on coffee. Jack looked around at the men. "Wonder why Ned an' Sully ain't back."

Gaylon said, "Knowin' Sully, they're layin' up with some woman. I'd like to know if they was able to pick up any pokes last night."

"Yeah an' if they did, they'd better not ah blowed it all on women."

****

Shorty had gone out to talk with Delbert. "Looks like we have all we need to start arresting robbers and outlaws. Every living soul in this town knows who they are. I've seen the biggest part of um. I'd like you to go with me to meet the mayor. I want the key to the jail and by damn he can appoint a sheriff an' at least one deputy."

"By darn Shorty, we've been trying to get him to do that for months. All he does is stall and mumble."

"Then I'd say it's time for you to show up at the No Scum Allowed Saloon and you men appoint another mayor."

"By darn if he won't do something after you talk with him, I'll get Arnold to go with me and we will do just that late this afternoon. I guess we should have already done it."

They rode in and Delbert said, "Well at least it looks like he's in his office."

They walked in and Delbert introduced Shorty and the mayor. Mayor Dudley looked at Shorty saying, "I sure as hell don't have any idea what you can do by yourself."

"I won't be by myself as soon as you appoint a sheriff and at least one deputy."

"This town doesn't have that kind of money! I'll look around and see if I can pick up someone that would want to be a deputy. A sheriff would cost too much."

Shorty said, "Where'll I find the keys to that jailhouse an' cells?"

"I have the keys to the jail, but the cell keys are hanging on a peg beside the door before going to the cells."

"Hand it to me."

"I will not! You are not law in this town! You are…"

Shorty had him by the shirt collar and six inches off the floor. "I wadn't askin' Partner, I was tellin. You shor's hell don't want'a be my first lock up."

As the mayor handed him the keys he said, "I'll have you arrested! You can't come in here and manhandle the town mayor and get away with it!"

"I'd say before you do that, you'd have to appoint ah sheriff. That's what this whole town wants an' needs."

Delbert and Shorty walked out, getting their horses and

leading them up the street. They opened that front door and Shorty said, "First thing is we need to hire somebody to dung this place out! Damn how long has it been closed up?"

"Ever since that county deputy sheriff quit and left town. It was either that or be killed."

"Smart feller. I guess you'd know who you can get to clean this place."

"Yes, my daughter and we'll ask Wanda Jorden if she wants to help. We'll see her in church tomorrow."

"Dad gum, this is Saturday. I guess there'll be a hell of ah lot goin' on tonight."

"Yes, all women and children stay off the streets from two hours before sundown. Have you thought of who you're going after first?"

"Yeah, that Billy Wilson an' his bunch. They're always in that Golden Spike Saloon."

"Think you'll need help?"

"I shor could use some, but I'll get er done. I'm not idiot enough to try an' face um all at once. But I'd bet ah nickel this place is at least half full between nine an' midnight."

"I'll go home and get Roberta to ride over and get

Wanda, they can have this place cleaned up in a couple hours."

"I'll not do much until after supper tonight an' well after dark. It'll take them ol' boys a while to drink enough they have to go to the outhouse. Then I'll get um."

Around three in the afternoon, the No Scum Allowed Saloon was already filling up, even Ray and Gerald were having a beer, getting ready for a big night.

Back at Willie's place, Gaylon and Jack were getting worried about Sully and Ned not getting back. Jack asked, "Think maybe that shooter got um".

"Could'a, I guess. Let's send one man in an' see if he can find um."

Jack looked around, "Darby, get to town an' nose ah round. Don't go in some saloon an' get drunk. Just find out where'n the hell they are an' get on back."

As he rode into town, Shorty walked into the No Scum Allowed just in time to hear Ray and Gerald tell about the gold robbery. One fellow asked, "What er you gonna do now?"

"Hunt um down like the low life skunks they are. We saw ever damn one of um and'll get um one er two at ah time."

Shorty walked over, "Raise yore right hands."

"What in the hell are you talkin' about, Cowboy?"

"I'm U.S. Marshal Shorty Thompson an' need ah couple deputies for ah short while. I want one of you to guard any prisoners that I bring to the jail. The other'n will be with me tonight as we get um."

Every man in there said, "Yer the marshal we've been waitin' on! Well hell Cowboy, deputize all of us!"

"Naw, I don't need y'all shootin' each other. Two's all I need an' by damn we'll get er done."

Both Gerald and Ray both raised their hands. "Hell yeah, Marshal, we'll be glad to do it. This'll make it even quicker than us gettin' um. It might'a took us ah while."

"We're gonna sit ah round an' have ah beer er two then go eat supper. Roberta an' Wanda are gonna get that jailhouse cleaned up this afternoon. Might be done now. Oh, I don't got no badges fer y'all, but maybe there's ah sheriff's badge er two in that desk drawer."

As they drank beer waiting on supper time, Darby rode in and started glancing in saloons. He wound up at the Golden Spike and thought he'd ask Billy if he had seen Sully and Ned. "Yeah, they tried robbin' a miner last night an' got shot. Both of um's deader'n hell. Then ah little cowboy shot one of my boys in the gun hand an' robbed um."

"Ah cowboy done that!?"

"Shor's hell did an'..."

"Think he could'a shot Sully an' Ned?"

"The boys said no, he wadn't tote'n no rifle an' they was shot with ah rifle. Blowed holes plumb thru um."

"Damn, guess I'd better get on back an' let Jack an' Gaylon know. Rifle you said, sounds like that hooded rider ah gain. That little skunk shor has got ah bunch ah us."

Billy said, "Yeah, got four ah my men. Soon's ever small miner an' that little cowboy is killed, that crap will stop. I'm hopin' to put ah end to that cowboy tonight. He walks thru that door, he's dead on the spot."

"Yeah, if him er the hooded rider don't get us all first."

"By damn they ain't gettin' us. There's seven of us left an' we're stickin' together. Jack an' Gaylon can run if they want to, not me. This town is where I get my gold."

"I'll go an' get out yonder an' let um know about Sully an' Ned. Guess we'll be in around dark, being as this is Saturday. There'll be miners in here lookin' fer poker games. Takin' their money at the poker table beats the hell out'a thumpin' um. That way they can go dig some more."

As he rode back to Willie's, Shorty, Ray and Gerald walked up to the sheriff's office. They walked in on two girls working away. Roberta looked up from moping the last cell and said, "Mister Shorty, we were just finishing up. Oh, this is Wanda Jorden, my best friend."

"And this is my help, Ray Wolfe and Gerald Holland. We're hopin' tonight we get this jail at least half full."

Wanda asked, "Are you going to take them over to Lincoln for trial?"

"I'll get a judge to hold trial right here in White Oaks being as this is where they have murdered an' robbed."

Wanda smiled, "I'd sure like to be on the jury. Which gang are you going to start with?"

"Any of um we see, but I'd say Billy Wilson an' his bunch will be the easiest got. They all hang out at the Golden Spike. When they go to the outhouse one er two at ah time, we'll get um ah Gerald er Ray can bring um to jail."

Roberta said, "We had better get on home. It will be supper time before we know it. I sure wish you three good luck and stay safe we need you. This town needs you."

Wanda said, "If you have to, just kill them. They have

hurt too many people."

Shorty said, "Our main thing is catch um, it'll be up to the judge an' jury as what they do with um."

The girls left and Shorty told Ray, "See if you can find the key to that gun cabinet and get them shotguns loaded."

They were just about ready to go eat when thru the door walked the mayor. He screamed, "I want everyone of you out of here! You have to authority to…"

Shorty smiled, "Lock him up Gerald. That sucker just might go blabbin' what we're up to an' get us killed."

"You! You can't do that! I am the mayor!"

"Get in that damn cell! You keep mouthin' off by damn I'll gag and hog tie you!"

As that cell was locked, Shorty said, "If yer a nice boy an' cause no trouble, I'll let you out where you can go home to supper. You raise hell you'll be there 'til we need the room. Us three are going to clean up yore lawless town. Then the good folks can vote you out'a office er keep you. That'll be up to them."

They walked out and over to the café. Ray said, "I shor can't see ah mayor not want'n robbin' an' killin' to stop in his town. Looks like the folks would'a showed him the road ah hell of ah long time ah go."

As they were eating, a meeting was going on in the No Scum Allowed Saloon. Delbert and Arnold had the town people all worked up. "Fellows, as you know we now have a U.S. Marshal helping us and he appointed Ray and Gerald as deputy U.S. Marshals so he now has men he could depend on. If they get in over their heads, how many of you are willing to help?"

"Hell Delbert, you know we'll all help. We may have to tie Mayor Dement to a chair someplace but we sure as hell can do that."

Another man said, "We can tell him to get his butt home an' stay there 'til it's all over. We know there's at least three big gangs an' no tellin' how many smaller ones that we hadn't noticed yet. This is gonna take that marshal some time. I just hope the hell them three can stay alive long enough to get it done."

Darby rode up and just stopped his horse close to the door. He could smell food and sure was hungry. He walked in and Jack asked, "Well?"

"They both was got while robbin' ah miner. I'd say got by the hooded rider being as they both was got with ah rifle. Then some little cowboy upped an' robbed ah couple of Billy's boys."

"What?"

"Yeah, shot one of un in his gun hand an' robbed um."

Gaylon laughed, "Now that has to be one tough little sucker! I wonder if he's got his self ah gang an's movin' in on us. We shor don't need somethin' like that, it cuts down on our take."

Jack said, "We might just have to do somethin' about that."

Gaylon asked, "Y'all goin' into town tonight?"

"Well yeah! It's Saturday an' there'll be ah lot ah money in town. Ain't y'all goin'?"

"Naw, too many gangs in there at one time might upset folks. Any of my men that want'a ride ah long can. I think just fer the hell of it I'm gonna hold off."

Jack smiled, "Not ah afraid that hooded shooter'll get you."

"Naw not really, I just have a bad feelin' somethin' is about to happen I wouldn't like. Fact is me an' my boys might just ride out'a here in ah few days."

"Oh. that'll be good, it'll leave more for me an' my boys. He laughed and said, "Alright everybody that's goin, let's get horses saddled."

All of Jacks men walked out and three of Gaylon's

looked at him. "Then you don't mind us going?"

"Naw, might do you good to have ah woman an' ah few drinks. I just don't feel up to it. We might ride in, in ah few hours, er not."

Shorty, Gerald and Ray went back over to the jail and unlocked that cell for the mayor. "Mayor if I was you, I'd get my butt home an' stay there. Tonight, there's one hell of ah chance bullets are gonna fly."

The mayor hot footed it out that door without saying a word. He was afraid that marshal would lock him up again. He headed for the No Scum Allowed Saloon. This town needed to know a U.S. Marshal had taken over the jail.

He walked in and called for quiet. "I thought you every-one should know, there's a U.S. Marshal in town! An…"

"The hell you say! How'd you find that out?"

"He locked me in a cell for over an hour."

Arnold said, "I'll get right over and tell him to get out of town! What the hell was he thinking, turning you loose?"

"No, I mean… What do you mean turning me loose? I should have never been locked up to start with."

"Mayor, ever since you was voted in, you have been nothing but a thorn to any law. We just voted you out, you are no longer mayor, so don't let that marshal bother you."

"You, you can't do that!"

"Like hell! We voted you in and voted you out as an inept mayor. We appointed Jeff Gall to fill in as mayor until we can have an' election. How about a drink to calm your nerves?"

"Hell no! I'm going home to supper!"

After the ex-mayor left, Delbert said, "Alright, everyone get home and get your guns and be back here within a half hour. If that marshal needs help, he damn sure knows where he can get it."

It was now dark and Jack and his men slowly rode in and tied up in front of the Little Casino Saloon. La Belle saw them walk in and hollered over. "I didn't know if you fellows would be in or not."

"Why not! It's Saturday night an' I see yer already busy."

"There's a U.S. Marshal in town."

"So? What can one marshal do against all us. He'd be ah damn idiot to try anything at all. Get his self killed is ah bout what he'll do."

"Jack, you go to killing U.S. Marshals, you won't be long for this world and you should know that."

"Me! Oh no I'd not do it, I'd have it done," He laughed and headed for a table.

As they sat there laughing and drinking, into town rode the hooded rider and stopped a half block behind the Golden Spike Saloon. That back door was seen each time it opened and men walked out.

CHAPTER FIVE

Around nine Shorty and Ray walked around to the back of the Golden Spike Saloon. They got in the shadows because the moon was bright tonight. The hooded rider saw that and slowly backed that horse around the side of a building and headed to the back of the Little Casino.

The back door was well in view as well as the outhouse. A night of wait and see was now taking place behind the Little Casino, as well as the Golden Spike Saloon.

The wait wasn't all that long before two men walked from the back door of the Golden Spike, headed to the outhouse. They walked into the outhouse and the door closed behind them. Shorty moved to where the door would open toward him, blocking their view as they walked out. Ray was waiting at the side, with gun in hand.

As those two walked out and that door closed behind them, there stood Shorty. "Hold it boys, it's cocked. Raise um high an' you yell out, it'll be yore last yell."

Ray walked up behind and took their pistols and said, "I believe you boys know where the jail is, head that'a way an' please don't stumble, it would be yore last. A bullet would hit you in the back before you hit the ground."

"You'll not get away with this by damn! You just don't know who in the hell yer messin' with."

"Perhaps before you hang, you'd like to tell me. If all goes right yore boss will be joinin' you well before midnight."

"Who in the hell are you? We know damn good'n well you ain't law. This is ah town with none."

"Feller, you are talkin' to a deputy U.S. Marshal. Now get! Shorty I'll take um if you want to wait on ah couple more."

"Are you shor you can handle it?"

"Maybe not, but I'd shor bet this cocked double barrel shotgun can. They try somethin', I'll scatter guts a half block. You boys hear that, let's be nice now."

"Go to hell!"

As they walked off, Shorty again settled into the darkness. Down the street and behind the Little Casino, several men had gone to the outhouse, but none the hooded rider had seen before. At last, three men walked out that back door. With rifle at his shoulder, the hooded rider rode into sight. "You want to die, just go for a gun. Raise um high or go for it, matters not to me."

They stood there hands very high. "Now with your left hands, very slowly reach around and get those pistols and let them fall. Just one of you tries anything, you all die."

That was done and the rider said, "Now head for the jail house, you run, you die."

They got to the street just as Ray was walking past with his two. The hooded rider said, "Here's three more for you. I'll ride along just in case they want to try and jump you."

Ray laughed, "With both triggers pulled at once, it'd not happen, but thanks. I'll take you up on the company until I let Gerald know I've got five comin' in."

They got in front of the jail and Ray called out. "Gerald, come on out with shotgun cocked! I've got five of um."

As those men were walked inside, Ray turned, "Thanks little feller. An' for all you've done up to now."

As they all walked in, the hooded rider rode back down behind the Little Casino and waited. "Wait! That marshal is alone!" That horse was moved out fast and behind the Golden Spike they went. "Hold it Marshal, don't shoot me I'm on your side. I just handed three of Slaughter's men over to Ray and they are in jail."

Shorty said, "Then you know we just got two of Billy's men. Any idea how many he still has?"

"Counting him, five. What do you say I go in that front door and you go in the back? I'll get their attention and you get Billy. We'll have to shoot the others because they will go for their guns."

"I'd like to get ah couple more of um 'fore I tried somethin' like that. Bullets comin' my way scares the hell out'a me."

"Then why don't I send a few bullets thru those front windows? They'd run over each getting out that back door right into your gun."

"No! I don't want'a kill um less I just have to. Thanks for yore help, but no."

"Okay Marshal, I have other things to do." The rider rode off and was out of sight in few seconds. The rider had been right, in both saloons, men were wondering what was taking their men so long to go to the outhouse. Billy said, "Orval, you'd better go out back an' take ah look. See if they're layin' out there dead."

"Billy, you can go straight to hell!"

Billy pushed back his chair and stood. "What did you say?"

"You can go straight to hell! You want'a check on um by damn do it yore self."

"Are you ah damn coward?"

"Hell yes, I'm ah coward! The thought of a bullet to the

chest scares the hell plumb out'a me."

"Well son of ah… By damn I'll go see. We'd heard if there'd been any shots."

He walked out that back door, hand on the butt of his pistol. "Harley, y'all out there?"

"Yeah!" Came the answer from the dark over at one side."

"What the hell are you doin', playin' with yore selves?"

A forty-five was cocked, sticking in his left ear. "Just you breathe easy, I damn shor don't want to pull this trigger 'less I just have to."

Shorty, with his left hand reached and got Billy's pistol from the holster. "Now lets me an' you take ah little walk up to the jailhouse 'fore yore boys get brave an' come lookin' for you. I hadn't had to kill nobody tonight, I'd shor hate it if you was my first."

Shorty shoved him and they headed from behind that building. The hooded rider came back down and was beside the building across the street, in total darkness.

Shorty got Billy to jail and Ray smiled, "I wanted to come on back down, but thought I might be seen."

"Well by dog there's still four more of um, let's go get

um."

At that very moment in that saloon, Orval stood. One of the men asked, "You goin' to check on Billy?"

"Hell no, I'm ridin'. He'd be back if he wadn't got."

Out that door four men went. As soon as all four were well away from that door, a voice called out, "You move or go for a gun you are dead!"

"Bull sh...' As he grabbed, he was knocked back into that wall and another cartridge was in that firing chamber.

That voice yelled "Next!"

Hands shot into the air. "Stand there, Marshal Shorty should have heard that shot."

And they did, Shorty and Ray were in a run and saw those three men standing there, hands raised. Both Shorty and Ray had their guns out, wondering what the hell those men were doing. "Y'all waitin' on us?"

"You Marshal Shorty?"

"Yeah."

"Then yer who we're waitin' on."

Shorty saw the dead man. "What happened to him?"

"Didn't believe the hooded rider."

"Where?"

"Over yonder… Damn, he's gone."

As those four were walked to jail, the hooded rider was back watching the Little Casino. A man from the Golden Spike ran up the street and into the Little Casino. "Billy an' his whole bunch was got! Only one of um was shot right out front. Them others an' Billy are in jail."

Jack jumped to his feet. "Time to ride boys!"

From across the street, the hooded rider took a bead on the first one to mount, but lowered that rifle. "Now that would have been dumb. I'll just follow them and see where they are holed up. I'd say these old boys will he headed out of this country as soon as they get up in the morning. Yes, maybe without coffee or breakfast."

That rider rode in the shadows as much as possible and stayed way back. Mostly listening to the sound of hoof beats. A mile or so later they stopped. Then a ride around and thru trees where a large house was seen backed up against the mountain and several horses were in the corral.

That's where those men took their horses then all went

inside. "So, this is where their hideout is. That marshal will have to know this. I think these suckers are in the running mood." The rider turned back for town.

In that house, Jack wasn't holding anything back. He told of Billy and his whole gang getting caught. "After we eat a bite in the morning, I'm gettin' the hell out'a here. I'd say that marshal has one hell of ah bunch ah help."

Gaylon said, "Yep boys time to find new territory for ah good spell. All good things come to ah end. We'll be headed out with y'all. The best thing is none of um know where we're at. We'll be long gone' fore they ever find this place, if they ever do."

Twenty minutes later, the hooded rider was in front of the jailhouse and hollered to see if the marshal was in there."

Shorty walked out, "I guess you had to kill that one back in front of the Golden Spike."

"I did, I gave them every chance to stand with their hands up until you got there. That one didn't believe me and went for his gun. How many men can you have ready to ride a half hour before sunup?"

"No idea, why?"

"I followed Jack Slaughter and his gang right to the house where the Swayne gang is staying. There are at least sixteen men left, could be even more as I could see in the barn."

"How do you know that?"

"After Jack and his men put their horses in the corral with a bunch more, I counted sixteen in all, unless some were in the barn or lying down where I couldn't see them."

"Where's it at? I'll get the men."

"Oh no you don't, I won't tell I'll lead you out there in the morning. I want to be in on the finish of this. I'll be right here an' hour before sunup."

As the hooded rider rode off, Shorty told Ray and Gerald he was headed for the No Scum Allowed to see how many of those men would ride with them before sunup.

When he got there, he saw every man in the place had a rifle or shotgun. "We've jailed all of the Billy Hart gang. The hooded rider follered Slaughter an' his bunch to a hideout where he thinks the Swayne gang is stayin'. He said it was no more than ah mile an' ah half. If we surround that place before sunup, I think we can put an end to these gangs once and for all."

And the answer was, "We'll ride with you Marshal."

Shorty looked around, seeing three elderly men. You,

you and you. Y'all have wives at home?"

Two of them did so Shorty said, "Then I shor wish you wouldn't go ah long. What would happen to them if you happened to get shot? Best you think of them first."

Those two looked at each other then one said, "Yer right Marshal, they couldn't get by without us."

Then Shorty asked, "Any of you here that has a wife with child? If so, we can get by without you."

Only one fellow said yes, his wife was due to give birth at any time. "I wadn't thinkin' Marshal, Winnie will be needin' me. I'll hold off goin' an' wish y'all luck."

"The rest of you be in front of the jail an hour before sunup in the mornin'. One other thing, when the shootin' starts, none of y'all stand up thinkin' you can get ah better shot. Shoot from cover only. If ah few of um happens to get away, so be it. I'll get them later I want ever one of y'all comin' back alive. If I say somethin' listen, it could save yore life. Now ever body get on home an' get yore sleep."

The next morning as they all met in front of the jail, those outlaws out at Willie's were just getting up and walking outside to do their morning duty. Jack asked, "Alright Gaylon, when'll we be ready to ride?"

"It's ah hell of ah long ride to anywhere. We'd better get

coffee on an' eat us one hell of ah breakfast. Then we'll get these horses saddled an' hook um."

"I'd say while ah couple are cookin' breakfast, the rest of us can have all the horses saddled."

"That'll work, after we have ah cup ah coffee."

They walked back in and two men already had a fire going in the cookstove and a huge coffee pot two thirds full of water. "How long 'fore that coffee's ready?"

"Hell, I don't know water's heatin'. Maybe ten er fifteen minutes it'll be ready."

Gaylon said, "I'll be back, I'm going out yonder an' take ah crap." He headed straight to the barn and that stall where their loot was hidden.

He grabbed a shovel, walked into that stall and pushed his horse out of the way. Three minutes later, that gold was in his saddle bags. He smiled, "Socorro here we come."

He walked back in and was handed a cup of coffee. Shorty and twenty-one men were well on their way. The hooded rider was between Shorty and Delbert. Shorty asked, "Don't you think it's about time you got rid of that hood?"

"When we get in position surrounding that house."

Shorty looked over, "Do you know any place to shoot except a feller the heart? I want all of um alive we don't just have to kill."

"Marshal, I can hit a dime as far away as I can see it. Just tell me where you want them shot. An ear, between the eyes, maybe a leg or arm."

"Just try not to kill um 'less you have to."

Fifteen minutes later they were all set. Shorty said, "If we can we want um all out'a that house an' at the corral. Then try to keep um from gettin' back in that house."

"One fellow asked, "What about the barn? Might be more horses in there an' fer all them had no room."

"The barn, sooner er later we could take. That house I'd say they have food an' water. That could take ah long time."

Undercover they waited, Shorty said, "I just hope they all come out'a that house at about the same time."

A young fellow of twenty or so said, "I can get um out'a there dad gum quick an' pretty near all at once."

"How's that?"

"That smoke comin' out'a that chimney. I'll unsaddle my horse an' ride over standing on his back an' put my saddle blanket over that chimney."

"Hell yeah, that'll work. Alright, when that's done ever body be ready. As much smoke it that is it'll not take um long."

He looked at the hooded rider who was behind a very large boulder. That hood was removed and the girl flipped her long black hair where it flowed over her shoulders. She smiled at Shorty.

"Wanda Jorden! Be damn, I'd never thunk it!"

Every man looked her way and smiled. One man said, "I ought'a knowed it! Them men hurt that girl one too many times. Mighty proud of you Wanda. Time to get even."

Before Shorty could say anything, she did, "Marshal, if you had known who I was before, you would have tried sending me home. I said I would be in on the last of this. Jimmy just put his saddle blanket over that chimney. You'd better quit looking at me and watch that front door.

It wasn't five minutes before everyone in the house started coughing and ran for the door. Jack was asking, "What in the hell did you do with that stove?"

Outside Ray and Gerald were side by side and said, "Leave Gaylon Swayne to us. Don't get me wrong, he'll live, just going to have ah few bullet holes in him."

With none of those outlaws being able to see through teary eyes, three minutes later five were dead and six wounded. The others just raised their hands and stood there, coughing and wiping tears. Shorty's men were on them in nothing flat.

Wanda, with rifle at ready walked over to Tom Olson, "Remember me?"

"Yeah, yer that..." She kicked him right under the chin.

"That will teach you to never grab a girl again. If not for Marshal Shorty, you would be dead and I would be spitting on your body."

All those men were lined up, sitting flat on their bottoms in the dirt. The wounded were looked after as other men saddled all the horses. Wilber came walking from the barn saying, "Ray, I'd guess this belongs to Mister Baxter."

"It does." He opened that sack and smiled, Wanda, please come over here."

She walked over, "Yes?"

"Here this five-pound gold bar is yours. Without you Girl, it would have taken a lot longer, then maybe we'd not got this back. Over time you cut um down to manageable size."

Gaylon had been shot in both legs and arms, but would live to hang. Jack was one that wasn't wounded and was saying, "I can't believe the hooded rider was a damn girl! Why in the hell did you do it?"

"Yours, Willie's and Billy's men hurt me one too many times. That last time I swore I'd see you all dead. And I will, you all will hang."

It was just before noon when those men were in jail or on the back porch of the undertaker with a blanket covering them. The cafes were full as everyone hadn't eaten since breakfast.

The new mayor walked in. He hollered, "I just wanted to let you folks and Marshal Thompson know, White Oaks is no longer a town with no law. I just appointed a sheriff and two deputies. Now that all the gangs are in jail, our town will once again be safe for everyone. Oh, Oh, one more thing, me and several of the men have decided to make August 1st a town holiday in honor of the hooded rider, Miss Wanda Jorden!"

Yells went up from everyone and Wanda was picked up and set on strong shoulders. They let her duck her head as they went out that door and down the street and back.

When they got back to the café, right out front was her dad, Arnold. Those men bent down so she just stepped off in front of her dad. "Ah dad I…"

He pulled her close, "I know dear, you had to do it and I'm proud of you. Because of you and Marshal Shorty we have law again, in a town known as a town with no law."

ABOUT THE AUTHOR

Paul L. Thompson

Born and raised on a farm and ranch in New Mexico, I only use true locations in all my novels. The name of towns are the same as in the 1880's, some are now ghost towns while others grew into our modern cities of today.

NOVELS FROM PAUL L. THOMPSON

(#101) U.S. Marshal Shorty Thompson - White Oaks - A Town With No Law

(#100) U.S. Marshal Shorty Thompson – Five Thousand Dollars

(#99) U.S. Marshal Shorty Thompson – Caught One Crooked Banker

(#98) U.S. Marshal Shorty Thompson – A Bad Decision

(#97) U.S. Marshal Shorty Thompson – The Last Man

(#96) U.S. Marshal Shorty Thompson - Gold and Silver – A Robber's Paradise

(#95) U.S. Marshal Shorty Thompson – Marshal Shorty Please Help Us

(#94) U.S. Marshal Shorty Thompson - Keith Aurzada - Lawyer Gunfighter

(#93) U.S. Marshal Shorty Thompson - Cimarron River - Rustlers Hideout

(#92) U.S. Marshal Shorty Thompson - The Fifth Man

(#91) U.S. Marshal Shorty Thompson - A Bit Of Crooked Law

(#90) U.S. Marshal Shorty Thompson - You Get Five Years

(#89) U.S. Marshal Shorty Thompson - A Kidnapped Education

(#88) U.S. Marshal Shorty Thompson - She's Alive, Not For Long

(#87) U.S. Marshal Shorty Thompson - Six Years Wait For A Showdown

(#86) Two Sister's Revenge

(#85) U.S. Marshal Shorty Thompson - Clayton New Mexico

(#84) U.S. Marshal Shorty Thompson - If Hell Ain't Hot Enough

(#83) U.S. Marshal Shorty Thompson - Mister You Was Shot In The Head

(#82) U.S. Marshal Shorty Thompson - Ms. Deborah Has Been Kidnapped

(#81) U.S. Marshal Shorty Thompson - One Sweet Kiss Can Kill You

(#80) U.S. Marshal Shorty Thompson - We're Gonna Die Ain't We Danny

(#79) You Shot Me Once! Never Again!

(#78) U.S. Marshal Shorty Thompson - Bartie Longshore - I Sentence You To Twenty Years

(#77) U.S. Marshal Shorty Thompson - Animas City - A Town to Forget

(#76) U.S. Marshal Shorty Thompson - Mister I'll See You Dead

(#75) U.S. Marshal Shorty Thompson - Don't Ever Make Old Men Mad

(#74) U.S. Marshal Shorty Thompson - Deputy U.S. Marshal Betty McCabe

(#43) A Very Long Time Before Cowboys

(#42) Long Trail To Nowhere

(#41) U.S. Marshal Shorty Thompson - You Think I Shot Him

(#40) U.S. Marshal Shorty Thompson - Revenge of the Bullet

(#39) U.S. Marshal Shorty Thompson - Killers and Outlaws

(#38) U.S. Marshal Shorty Thompson - Little Toby Smith

(#37) Love Is One Shadow Away

(#36) U.S. Marshal Shorty Thompson - Hang Shorty in Leadville, Colorado

(#35) Young Outlaws (almost)

(#34) U.S. Marshal Shorty Thompson - Doug Brown & Shelly Hampton

(#33) William Colby U.S. Marshal Retired

(#32) U.S. Marshal Shorty Thompson - The Road To Chama

(#31) U.S. Marshal Shorty Thompson - Milo Tillie

(#30) U.S. Marshal Shorty Thompson - James P. Retzer - Dentist - New Mexico, Territory

(#29) U.S. Marshal Shorty Thompson - Janice McCord Rides Again

(#28) U.S. Marshal Shorty Thompson - David Graham - The New Gun

(#27) U.S. Marshal Shorty Thompson - Please Don't Leave Me

(#26) U.S. Marshal Shorty Thompson - Cowboy Cody Strickland

(#25) U.S. Marshal Shorty Thompson - The Martin Boys

(#24) Before I Die

(#23) U.S. Marshal Shorty Thompson - Killing Of Outlaws

(#22) U.S. Marshal Shorty Thompson - Whiskers McPherson & Gabriel O'Grady

(#21) U.S. Marshal Shorty Thompson - Janice McCord

(#20) U.S. Marshal Shorty Thompson - This Mountain Is Mine

(#19) U.S. Marshal Shorty Thompson - The Young Trackers

(#18) U.S. Marshal Shorty Thompson - The Wrong Man Again

(#17) U.S. Marshal Shorty Thompson - The Long Chase For Justice

(#16) The Last Gun in Town

(#15) U.S. Marshal Shorty Thompson - Women In The West Did Survive

(#14) U.S. Marshal Shorty Thompson - Young Jessie Owens

(#13) Brothers of The West

(#12) U.S. Marshal Shorty Thompson - When Preaching Is Hell

(#11) U.S. Marshal Shorty Thompson - A Mother's Wrath

(#10) Can Loneliness Last Forever

(#9) One Good Deed

(#8) U.S. Marshal Shorty Thompson - Children Of The West

(#7) U.S. Marshal Shorty Thompson – Malpais

(#6) U.S. Marshal Shorty Thompson - Ride Hard For Rayado

(#5) U.S. Marshal Shorty Thompson - Trouble in Tascosa

(#4) Saddle Mountain

(#3) U.S. Marshal Shorty Thompson - Willow Lane

(#2) U.S. Marshal Shorty Thompson - Silver of the Black Range

(#1) U.S. Marshal Shorty Thompson

thompsonpaull@outlook.com

www.oldwestnovels.com

www.longhornpublishing.com

info@longhornpublishing.com

Printed in Great Britain
by Amazon